Congratulations! I have enjoyed watching you both during your adventure. I can't wait to meet little Miss Gentry, she will be loved beyond measure.

When I chose a book, it had to be something that would help instill passion in her heart. When I found this book about our Indiana Hoosiers, I knew it was the one.

Much love to you both
&
Go Hoosiers!

Love,
Heather

# HOO-HOO-HOO HOOSIERS!

Story by Terry Hutchens

Illustrations by Phil Velikan

TERRY HUTCHENS PUBLICATIONS

**HOO HOO HOO HOOSIERS! © 2016 Terry Hutchens**

Layout, cover and digital illustrations by Phil Velikan www.FindPhil.com

Edited by Holly Kondras
Packaged by Wish Publishing

Printed in the United States of America
10 9 8 7 6 5 4 3 2 1

Published by Terry Hutchens Publications
TerryHutchensPublications.Com

Watercolor llustration
©2016 Anna Timke

This book is dedicated to the next generation of

# Hoo-Hoo-Hoo Hoosiers!

"Mommy! Can you come here for a minute?"

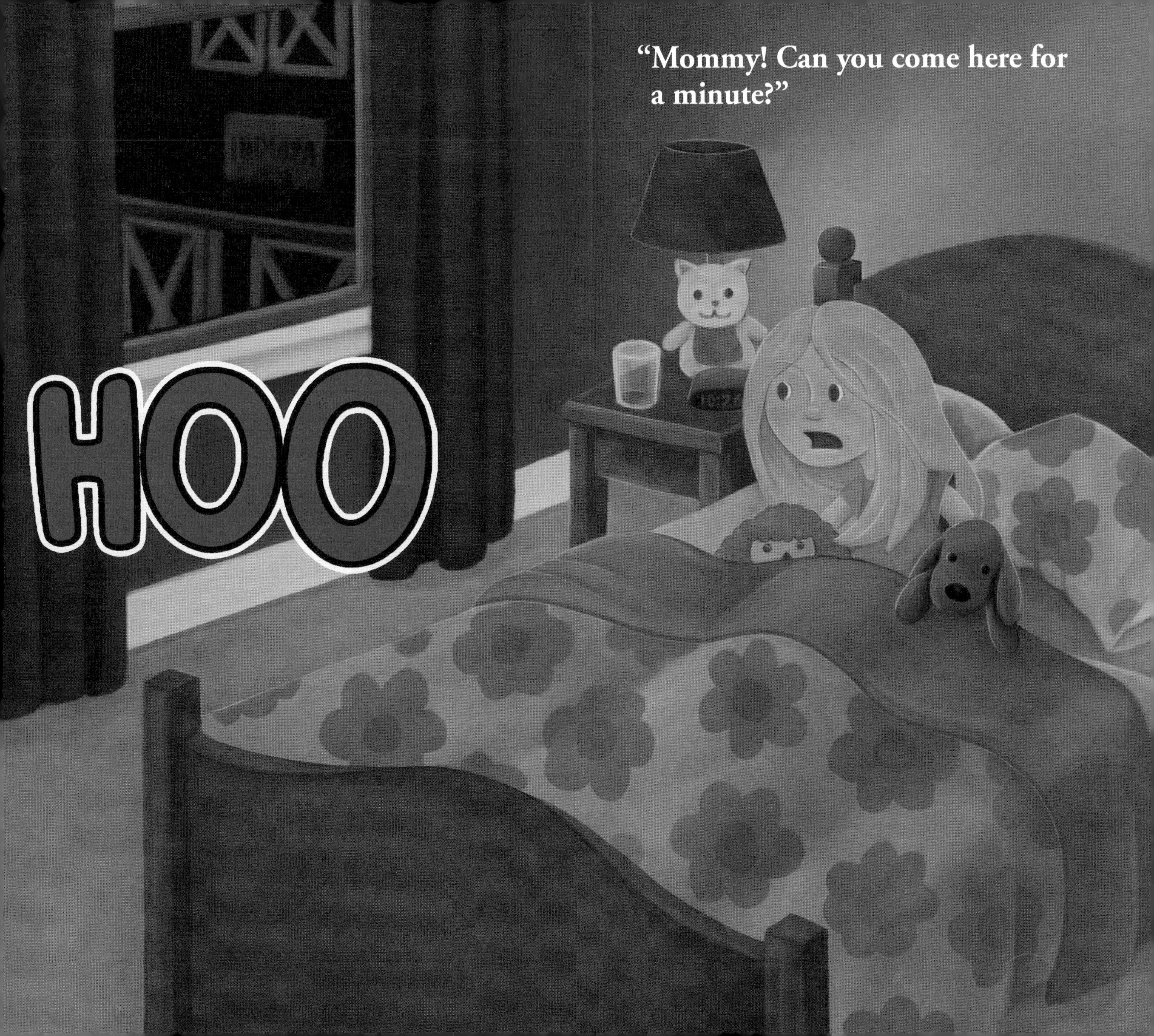

"What's the matter, Jenny?"

"I heard a noise. It went 'Hoo-Hoo-Hoo.' What is it?"

"I don't know, sweetie. Did it come from outside?"

# WHOOOO

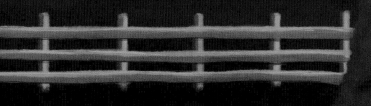

"Is that the sound you heard, Jenny?"

"No, that's not it."

CHOOOO CHOOOO

"Is that the sound you heard, Jenny?"

"No, that wasn't the sound either."

"Maybe the sounds you're hearing are
  coming from the barn, Jenny. Let's go see."

"OK."

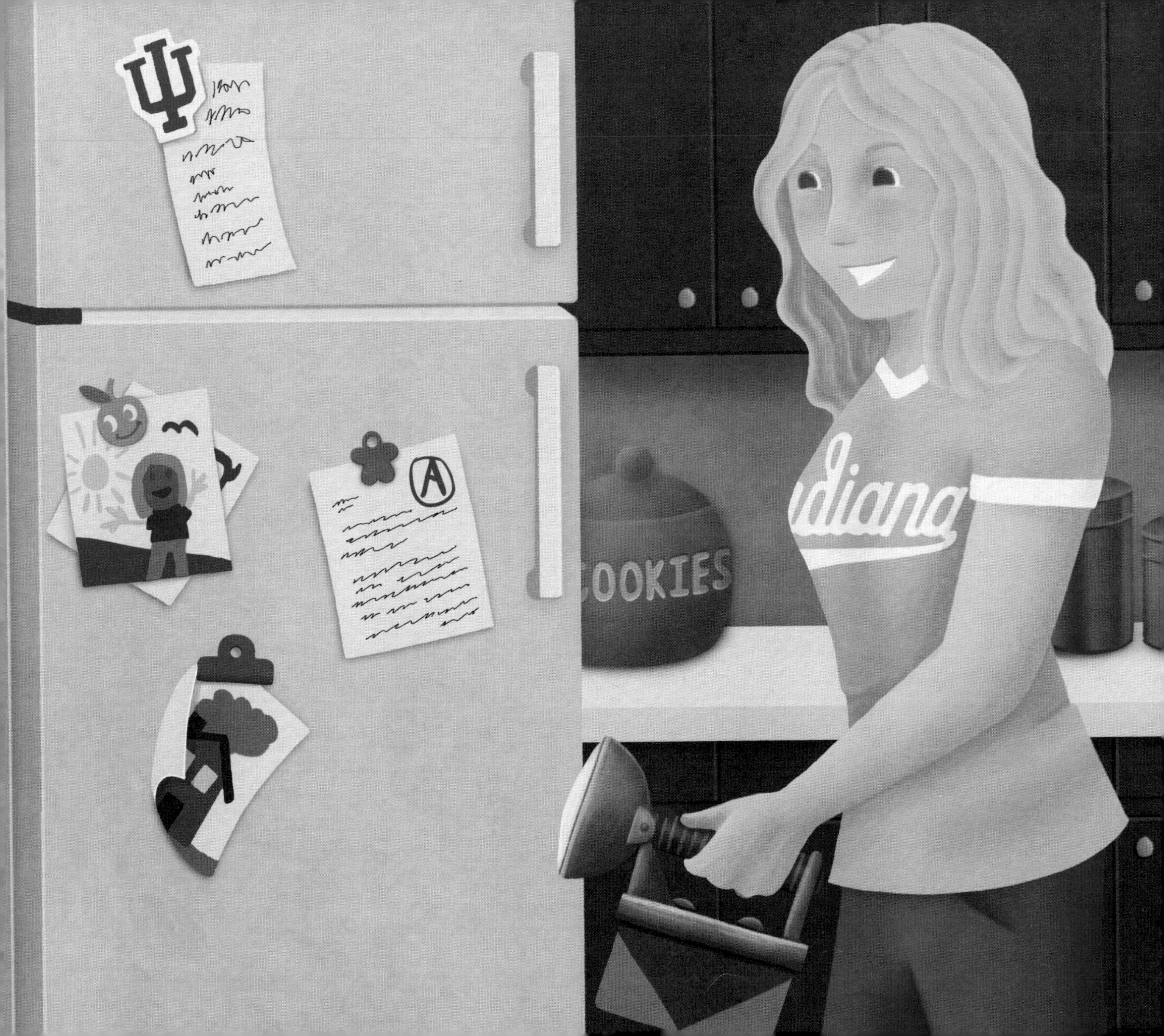
A
COOKIES

"Is that the sound you heard, Jenny?"

"No, it was more of a 'Hoo' than a 'Moo.' "

"Hi Grandpa."

"Hey, sweet thing. What are you doing still awake?"

"I've been hearing a noise and I can't figure out what it is. It sounds like 'Hoo-Hoo-Hoo.' Do you know what it could be? "

CHOOOO-CHOOOO

WHOOO WHOOO WHOOO

MOOO MOOOO

"Could it have been an owl? There's one in that tree."

"No, Grandpa. That wasn't the right sound."

"Maybe you heard a train. A train kind of sounds like that, don't you think?"

"No, that wasn't the sound either."

"I bet it was a cow. They've been pretty loud tonight."

"No, it was not a cow. We checked."

"Well, I'm sure we'll figure it out. You go get some sleep now, Jenny. We'll see if we can find the answer tomorrow."

"I sure hope so. Good night, Grandpa."

"Is that the sound you heard, Jenny?"

"No, I know that's just Grandpa. That wasn't it either."

"Bless you, Grandpa!"

"Why are you still up, honey?' Isn't it past your bed time?"

"I've been hearing this noise, Daddy, and I can't figure out what it is. It's like 'Hoo-Hoo-Hoo.' Do you know what it could be?"

24
sports
ONE
team

"Do you think it might be an owl?"

"No, not an owl, Bryan."

"Could it have been a train or a cow?"

"No, it's not one of those, Kevin."

WHOOO WHOOO

CHOOO-CHOOO

MOOO MOOOO

"Your grandpa is sneezing a lot.
I think he has a cold."

"No, Daddy, that's not right either."

"How about a hot chocolate before you go back to bed? You've had a rough night."

"Thanks, Mommy. I just wish I could figure out that sound. I can't believe I haven't heard it again."

"I'm sure you'll hear it again, and we'll get it figured out."

"That's it! That's the sound I heard: Hoo-Hoo-Hoo."

"You heard the Indiana fans on the TV cheering for our basketball team. That's what they say when something good happens."

"Hoo-Hoo-Hoo Hoosiers!  I like to say that."

"Well, honey that's good because you're going to be hearing that a lot. Our family loves Indiana basketball, and we love the Hoosiers!"

"I love the Hoosiers, too, Daddy!"